The mice and the weasels

and other Aesop's Fables

Compiled by Vic Parker

Miles

First published in 2013 by Miles Kelly Publishing Ltd
Harding's Barn, Bardfield End Green, Thaxted, Essex, CM6 3PX, UK

2 4 6 8 10 9 7 5 3 1

Publishing Director Belinda Gallagher
Creative Director Jo Cowan
Editorial Director Rosie McGuire
Designer Joe Jones
Production Manager Elizabeth Collins
Reprographics Stephan Davis, Jennifer Hunt, Thom Allaway

ISBN 978-1-84810-940-7

Printed in China

British Library Cataloguing-in-Publication Data
A catalogue record for this book is available from the British Library

ACKNOWLEDGMENTS
The publishers would like to thank the following artists who have contributed to this book:
Cover: Marco Furlotti
Advocate Art: Natalie Hinrichsen, Tamsin Hinrichsen
The Bright Agency: Marcin Piwowarski
Frank Endersby
Marco Furlotti
Jan Lewis (decorative frames)

Made with paper from a sustainable forest

www.mileskelly.net   info@mileskelly.net

www.factsforprojects.com

Contents

The Wolf
and the Kid

Goats are very good at scrambling up and down steep mountainsides, climbing where others can't go.

Once upon a time, a kid clambered on top of a store shed in the farmyard and perched on the roof, looking down proudly on everyone below. Just then, a wolf slunk by, casting his eyes around greedily for a possible meal. Immediately, the kid began to tease and taunt the wolf – for he felt quite safe up on the roof.

"Mr Wolf," he cried. "You are a murderer and a

thief. I don't know how you dare show your face near the homes of honest folk. We know the crimes you commit!"

"Curse away, my young friend," said the wolf. "You are only being so bold because you know that I can't get my claws into you at the moment."

It is easy to be brave when you are a safe distance from danger.

The Bald Man and the Fly

It was a hot *summer's day* and a bald man who had finished work sat down under a shady tree to rest. How pleasant it was, relaxing in the cool. His eyelids began to droop and his head started to nod.

Just as the man was about to fall asleep, a fly began hovering round his head. Buzz! Buzz! Buzz! The man was very annoyed. Buzz! Buzz! Buzz! The fly zipped this way and that, darting forwards and stinging him here and there.

The bald man was hugely annoyed and began swatting at his enemy, aiming blow after blow at the buzzing creature. But again and again he missed, and his hand landed on his own head instead! Still the fly tormented him.

Finally the man gave up, allowing the fly to buzz where it liked. "I will hurt myself more than it is hurting me, if I carry on," he said to himself.

 If you seek to harm an enemy, you may only end up hurting yourself.

The Fisherman Piping

One day a fisherman had a new idea for how he might catch fish. He thought that if he took his flute to the riverbank and played a jolly tune, the fish might hear the music, and come to the surface and dance – making it easy for the fisherman to catch them.

So he began to play one merry tune after another, but not a single fish put so much as its nose out of the water. The fisherman gave up, laid down his flute, and went back to his old method of just casting his net into the water.

To his astonishment, when he drew the net in it was heavy with fish! Then the fisherman took up his flute and played again, and as he played, the fish flipped and flapped in the net.

"Ah, you dance now when I play," said he.

"Yes," replied an old fish, "now we have no choice."

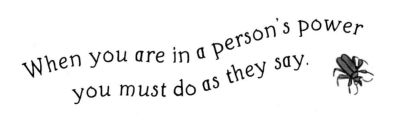

When you are in a person's power you must do as they say.

The Ants

ong ago, ants were once people and made their living by farming the land. However, people weren't content with the results of their own hard work. They were always looking longingly at their neighbors' crops, which seemed much better than their own. Whenever they could lay their hands on their neighbors' produce, they stole it, and hid it in their store houses.

In those days, the gods and goddesses of Mount Olympus ruled the world.

When father of the gods, Jupiter, saw how things had become, he was disgusted with humankind. He was so furious that he changed people into ants.

However, although their bodies changed, their nature remained the same. So to this day, people go about the cornfields and gather the fruits of others' labors, and store them up for their own use.

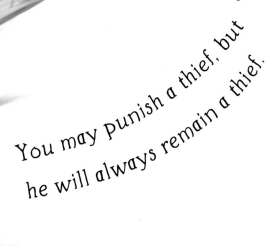

You may punish a thief, but he will always remain a thief.

The Mice
and the
Weasels

The mice and the weasels were sworn enemies, and there came a time when things got so bad that they went to war. They fought battle after battle, but the mice always came off the worst, with many being killed and eaten by the weasels.

At last the mice realized that they were near to being defeated once and for all. So they called a meeting to discuss if there was anything they could do that they had not already thought of, to avoid disaster. All of the oldest,

wisest mice were there, solemnly putting their heads together to try to think of plans. Then one old mouse got up to speak.

"It's no wonder we are always beaten, for we have no generals to plan our battles and direct the movements of our troops in the field."

This made a lot of sense to the other mice and they acted on his advice. They at once chose the biggest mice to be their generals. These mice, in order to be marked out as different from the foot soldiers, wore big helmets decorated with plumes of straw. The generals then led the mice to battle, confident of victory... however, they were defeated as usual.

Soon, all the mice were scampering as fast as they could back to their holes. They all made their way to safety without difficulty, except the generals. They couldn't squeeze into their

holes because their helmets were too broad and the plumes of straw on top were too tall. So they were left to the clutches of the weasels.

Greatness carries its own dangers and punishments.

The Bee and Jupiter

Long, long ago, when the world was very young, great gods and goddesses ruled the Earth from their home on Mount Olympus.

One day, a queen bee flew up to Olympus with some fresh honey from her hive. It was a present for the king of the gods, Jupiter.

Jupiter was highly pleased with the bee's thoughtful gift. In return, he promised to give the delighted queen bee anything she liked.

The insect thought hard – she did not want to waste such a wonderful reward. Finally, she

announced that she would be grateful to Jupiter if he would give stings to her and all her kind. Jupiter was taken aback by this, and asked why. The queen explained that it would allow them to sting people who stole their honey. Jupiter wasn't happy about this, for he loved humankind, but he had given his word. So he agreed. Yet the stings he gave were of such a kind that whenever a bee stings someone, the sting is left in the wound and the bee dies.

Evil wishes always come home to roost.

17

The Fir Tree
and the
Bramble

There was once a forest in which lived a very proud fir tree. She thought she was better than all the other trees, bushes and plants because she grew taller and straighter than anything else she could see.

One day she began boasting to a bramble, and said in a very snooty manner, "You poor thing, you are of no use whatsoever. Now, look at me – I am useful for lots of things. For instance, when people build houses, they always choose fir. They can't do without me."

18

The bramble wasn't upset at all. She cleverly replied, "Ah, that's all very well, but you wait until people come with axes to cut you down. Then you'll wish you were a bramble and not a fir."

It is sometimes better to be poor without any cares, than to be rich and weighed down with duties.

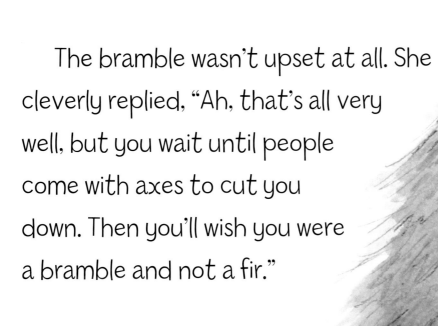

The Fly and the Mule

O nce upon a time, a mule was plodding slowly down a road, pulling a cart. A tiny fly suddenly appeared and sat on the edge of the cart.

"How slow you are!" said the fly. "Can't you go faster? I'm in a hurry! Speed up or I will use my sting as a whip."

However the mule was not in the least bit bothered. "Behind me in the cart," he said, "sits my master. He holds the reins and flicks me with his whip, and I obey him. I'm not going to take

any notice of your cheek. I know when I have to go fast and when it's better to go slow."

Life is not just about going at top speed.

21

The Fisher
and the
Little Fish

A fisher had once been fishing all day long and had caught nothing at all. Evening was about to draw in, but there was just time for the fisher to cast his nets one last time before going home.

When he drew the nets in, he saw that he had caught something at last. However, it was just a single little fish, which looked up at him and begged for mercy.

"Pray, let me go, master," said the fish. "I am much too small for you to eat just now. Look at

22

me – I am hardly going to make a bite, let alone a whole meal. If you put me back into the river, I shall soon grow much bigger, then you can make a splendid banquet of me."

But the fisher shook his head. "No no, my little fish," he said. "I am very lucky to have you now. Another time, I may not get you at all."

A little thing in the hand is worth more than a great thing that you do not have yet.

The Mountains in Turmoil

Once upon a time, a group of villagers built their homes around the base of some towering mountains.

The mountains were like giants – huge and threatening – but the villagers didn't want to move anywhere else because the earth around the mountains was rich, and crops grew well.

One day, smoke started to pour from the mountain tops, the earth began to quake and rocks came tumbling down. The people were terrified that the mountains had come to life.

They felt sure that something awful was happening. Everyone huddled together, convinced they were going to die.

Suddenly the earth shook violently and a huge gap appeared in the side of the mountains. The people fell to their knees and waited for the end to come.

At long last, a teeny tiny mouse poked its head and whiskers out of the gap and came scampering toward them.

And that was the end of it!

There is often much fuss about nothing.

The Lion
and the
Mouse

Once, a little mouse came upon a lion who was fast asleep. The mouse had never seen a lion close up before and was very curious to see what his great mane felt like. Very boldly, the mouse crept as nimbly as he could up the lion's leg, along his back, and all the way to his soft, thick mane. However, even though the mouse was being as light and quiet as he could, his movements woke the mighty beast.

As the mouse ran back down the lion's leg, an enormous paw clamped down upon his tail. Then

the lion snarled and opened his big jaws to swallow him.

"Pardon, oh King," cried the little mouse, trembling in terror. "Forgive me this time, and I shall never forget it. You never know, I may even be able to return the favour one of these days."

At this bold idea, the lion began to laugh. He was so amused at the thought of the mouse being able to help him that he let him go.

Some time after, the lion was unlucky enough to be caught in a trap. The rejoicing hunters wanted to carry their prize alive to show their king. So they bound the injured lion and tethered him to a tree while they went in search of a wagon to carry him on.

Just then, the little mouse happened to pass by, and recognized the lion at once. Seeing his sad plight, the mouse scampered straight up to him. It was only a few moments before he had gnawed away the ropes and the lion was free.

"You see?" said the little mouse. "Was I not right after all?"

Little friends may prove great friends.

The Eagle
and the
Beetle

Long ago, an eagle was chasing a hare, who was running for her life. She was at her wits end to know where to turn for help.

At last the hare saw a beetle and begged him to help her. Although the beetle was tiny, he swore he would do what he could to help.

The hare sank down exhausted, and the eagle swooped in for the kill. But the tiny beetle puffed up his chest and stood tall. He shouted to the eagle not to touch the hare, for she was under his protection. Of course the eagle never noticed the beetle – he was far too small. So the bird just seized the hare and ate her up.

The beetle never forgot this, and from then on he kept an eye on the eagle's nest. Whenever the eagle laid an egg, the beetle climbed up and rolled it out so that it broke. He remained quite

unseen by the eagle, who became desperate at the loss of all her eggs.

At last the eagle grew so worried over the loss of her eggs that she went to the great god Jupiter, who was the special protector of eagles.

"Please help me great Jupiter," begged the eagle. "I cannot bear to keep losing my eggs this way. I need a safe place in which to keep them."

The god took pity on the eagle and invited her to lay her eggs in his lap. There he could keep a close eye on them.

The beetle had been watching and listening to the eagle's pleas. Immediately, he made a ball of dirt the size of an eagle's egg, and flew up and placed it in Jupiter's lap. When Jupiter saw the dirt, he stood up to shake it out of his robe, and, forgetting about the eagle's eggs, he shook them out too.

The eggs were broken just as before. And ever since then, eagles never lay their eggs in the season when beetles are out and about.

The weak can always find ways to avenge an insult, even upon the strong.

The Lion, Jupiter and the Elephant

The lion, for all his size and strength, and his sharp teeth and claws, is a coward in one way – he can't bear the sound of a rooster crowing, and he runs away whenever he hears it.

Once, the lion complained bitterly to the great god Jupiter for making him like that, but Jupiter said it wasn't his fault and he had done the best he could for him. Jupiter also said that, considering this was the lion's only weakness, he ought to be content.

The lion, however, wouldn't be comforted,

and was so ashamed of his timidity that he prowled around with a heavy heart.

One day the lion met the elephant and the two got talking in friendly conversation. The lion noticed that the great beast cocked up his ears all the time, as if he were listening for something, and the lion couldn't resist asking why he did so. Just then a tiny fly came humming by, and the elephant said, "Do you see that horrible little buzzing insect? I'm terribly afraid that

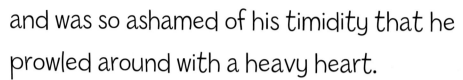

it will get into my ear — if it gets in, I'm done for. That's why I keep flapping my ears — to keep the little fly out of them."

The lion's spirits rose at once when he heard this. "For," he said to himself, "if the elephant, huge as he is, is afraid of a fly, I needn't be so much ashamed of being afraid of a rooster, which is ten thousand times bigger than a fly."

There is no shame in being afraid, no matter how big you are.

The Fly and the Lion

There was once a tiny fly who had no fear. He went striding up to a lion, who could barely see him, and said, "I am not in the least bit afraid of you. What does your strength amount to after all? I'm stronger than you. If you don't believe it, let us fight and see." With that, the fly sounded his battle horn, darted in and bit the lion's nose.

When the lion felt the sting, he was furious. However in his haste to swat the fly, he only succeeded in scratching his nose and making it

bleed. He failed
altogether to
hurt the fly,
which buzzed
off in triumph,
overjoyed.

The fly's
celebrations were
short-lived however.
It flew straight into a
spider's web, and was
caught and eaten by the spider. And so the fly
fell prey to an insignificant creature after having
triumphed over the King of the Beasts.

No one is so great that
they cannot fail.

The Mouse and the Bull

There was once a bull who was feeding on a bale of straw. He had no idea that a mouse was living there. The mouse was angry that the bull was about to destroy his home. As the bull lowered his head to eat, the tiny mouse bit the great animal on the nose. Cheekily, the mouse then disappeared into a hole in the wall.

Despite the surprise, the bull charged at the wall,

butting it with his huge head – but the wall held firm. After a while, the bull became tired and sank to the ground. Then, when all was quiet, the mouse ran out and bit him again!

The bull was beside himself. He rose to his feet, but the mouse ran back in the hole again, and the bull could do nothing but bellow and fume. Then he heard a shrill voice say, "You big fellows don't always have it your way – sometimes we little ones come off best."

The battle is not always won by the strong.